Q.T. Pie meets SMART E

By Stephanie Sanders
Illustrated by Galen T. Pauling

Published by The SanPaul Group, L.L.C., Detroit, Michigan 48219

™ and © 2003 Stephanie Sanders and Galen T. Pauling, The SanPaul Group, L.L.C. All rights reserved.
No part of this book may be reproduced or copied in whole or in part in any form without
written permission from the copyright owner. Q. T. Pie and Smart E are trademarks of
Stephanie Sanders and Galen T. Pauling. Printed in Singapore.
Library of Congress Catalog Card Number: 2003108130 ISBN: 0-9670875-4-6

"Mama! Mama!" Q. T. Pie shouted as she
looked out the kitchen window.
"Yes Q. T., what is it?" her mother replied.
"Some boy is going into Ms. Mary's house with a bunch of
suitcases and stuff, like he's going to be staying for awhile."

"Yes, and...?"
"Do you know who he is, Mama?"
"No Q. T. I don't, but I'm sure we'll know soon enough.
Now did you water my flowers like I asked you to, or
were you too busy being a busybody?"

"Ma, Ms. Mary hugged that boy so tight, I thought his head was going to pop off his body and go rolling down the street. She seemed so happy he had arrived."

"Maybe she is. He's probably special to her just like you're special to your dad and me. Now go outside and play with your friends, and don't forget to water my flowers."
"Alright."
"And stop being so nosy."

"Liz, some boy just showed up at Ms. Mary's House.
Do you know who he is?" asked Q. T.
"No, Q. T. I don't," Liz answered.

"Mommie, I'm going outside to play with Q. T., okay?"
(Spanish) "Mami, yo voy a jugar afuera con Q. T., bueno?"

"Have fun," her mom replied.
(Spanish) "Se divierte," su mamá contestada.

"Let's go and get Yasmina and play some double dutch.
Forget about the new boy. We'll know who
he is sooner or later," Liz said.

"I can't believe you don't want to know who
the new boy is," insisted Q. T.
Liz giggled.
"Well you can worry about the new boy if you want to,
but I'm ready to have some fun. Now come on."

"Hey Yasmina," Q. T. and Liz said simultaneously.
"Hey," Yasmina smiled.
"Where's the jump rope?" asked Liz.
"I have it right here," said Yasmina.

"Feet in," said Q. T.
Just as Liz was about to start the elimination game to determine who would go first, two more feet appeared.

Two voices said, "Hold it, we want to play."
The girls looked up from the two feet that suddenly got added
to the group, and there stood Wendell and Jerry.

"Now we have to start over," said Liz. "Eenie, meenie, miney, mo. Catch a tiger by his toe. If he hollers let him go. Eenie, meenie, miney, mo. Out goes the cat, out goes the rat, out goes the lady with the alligator hat."

"Wendell and Jerry do you know who the new boy at
Ms. Mary's is?" asked Q. T. while Liz was eliminating.
"No," said Jerry. "I saw the cab pull up this morning. Ms. Mary
sure looked happy to see him. We'll see him in school Monday."

"You're out, Wendell," said Liz.
"Yeah, we'll know who he is sooner or later," said Wendell.
"You're out, Q. T."
"You're out Yasmina."
"I'm always out when you do it, Liz. You always win first jump."

Liz and Jerry were left, and sure enough
Liz was the winner for first jump.
"Told you," said Yasmina. Every time you do Eenie, Meenie,
Miney Mo, you win. I'm doing it next time."
"That's fine, let's play," said Liz.

They played double dutch for a long time. Finally Yasmina's
mom called her in. Liz had to leave for her dance class. Jerry
and Wendell left with some friends to go ride their bikes on
Sissy Hill. Q. T. went to the store with her mother.

As Q. T. and her mother rode by Ms. Mary's, Q. T. shouted.
"There he is, Mama, sitting on the porch reading a
book! Why would he be reading a book when he
could be playing?" Q. T. wondered aloud.

"Maybe since he doesn't know anybody, he doesn't have anything he would rather be doing. Maybe he likes to read," Q. T.'s mother responded, a little agitated by her daughter's comment.

"Maybe he's real smart and goofy."
"Q. T. you don't have to be goofy to be smart.
Don't assume smart means goofy. Don't try to
judge him until you meet him; that's not nice."

"Do you think he'll be in school on Monday, Ma?"
"If Ms. Mary has anything to do with it, he'll
be in school on Monday."

Monday finally arrived. As Q. T. dressed for school, she wondered if she would see the new boy. None of her friends seemed to care, but she was curious.

Mrs. Adams, the teacher, called everyone's attention. "Children we have a new member to welcome to our class. Please come here young man and introduce yourself."

The new boy stood up and turned around.
"My name is Elias Ethic. Ms. Mary is my grandmother.
I am from Chicago, and I'm happy to be in Diver City."
"Thank you, Elias," said Mrs. Adams.
"You can all welcome Elias later. Now it is time for the lesson."

When Q. T. Pie arrived home from school, Mama told
her that they were invited over to Ms. Mary's
for dinner to meet her grandson.

Q. T. Pie was excited to be invited over to Ms. Mary's for dinner. She could really burn. That's the word Mama used when someone could cook really well. Elias was going to love eating Ms. Mary's food everyday. She could make Brussels sprouts taste good.

"Welcome," said Ms. Mary as she opened the door and graciously greeted Q. T. Pie and her family.

"Hi, Ms. Mary. Where's your grandson, Elias?" Q. T. Pie asked.
"Smart E's probably upstairs working on that computer of his.
Go on up and say hello."

When Q. T. got to Elias' room he was sitting in an old comfortable chair sideways, with his hat turned backward, reading a book.
"Hi Elias," said Q. T.
"Hello," replied Elias.

"My name is Quintessence. I'm in Mrs. Adams class with you."
"I'm very pleased to meet you, Quintessa."
"Quintessence. Everybody calls me Q. T."
"Your grandmother called you Smart E.
Is that what I should call you?"
"That's what everybody back in Chicago called me."

Soon they heard Jerry, Wendell, Liz, and Yasmina coming up
the stairs. Q. T. Pie introduced everybody to Smart E.
Ms. Mary soon called them all down for dinner.

As they went downstairs to dinner, Jerry and Wendell challenged
Smart E to ride Sissy Hill. He told them that as soon as his
bike arrived from Chicago, he'd ride any hill they wanted.
"Cool," said Jerry. They slapped each other a
high five and headed to the kitchen.

The food smelled wonderful. All the children bowed their heads to say grace before eating. Once they ate, they all went outside to play.

Everyone put their feet in for Eenie, Meenie, Miney, Mo. Liz tried to lead it again, when Yasmina stopped her. "Don't even try it Liz. Let Smart E do it." Smart E ended up being "It." The children had great fun.

They played until dark. Q. T. Pie waved goodbye
to Smart E as everyone headed home.
Smart E isn't goofy at all," Q. T. Pie told Mama.
"He was a lot of fun." Mama smiled, squeezing
Q. T. Pie's hand as they walked home.

Challenging Words!

Included with every Q. T. Pie Book will be words called Challenging Words to add to your vocabulary. The Challenging Words from this story are:

SIMULTANEOUSLY - (sī məl tā′ nē əs ly) Done at the same time.

ELIMINATION - (ē lim′ə ñat′ tion) To take out; remove; or get rid of.

AGITATED - (aj′itāt′id) To upset; to disturb or trouble.

COMFORTABLE - (kum′ fər tə bəl) Restful; at ease in body or mind.

WONDERFUL - (wun′ dər fəl) Very good, excellent.